W9-AAW-200

The Adventures of Sam X

THE SERPENT ON MY SKIN

by *Hubert Ben Kemoun*

illustrated by François Roca

translated by Genevieve Chamberland

Librarian Reviewer
Marci Peschke
Librarian, Dallas Independent School District
MA Education Reading Specialist, Stephen F. Austin State University
Learning Resources Endorsement, Texas Women's University

Reading Consultant
Elizabeth Stedem
Educator/Consultant, Colorado Springs, CO
MA in Elementary Education, University of Denver, CO

STONE ARCH BOOKS
MINNEAPOLIS   SAN DIEGO

First published in the United States in 2008
by Stone Arch Books,
151 Good Counsel Drive, P.O. Box 669
Mankato, Minnesota 56002
www.stonearchbooks.com

Library of Congress Cataloging-in-Publication Data
Ben Kemoun, Hubert, 1958–
   [Monstre dans la peau. English]
   The Serpent on My Skin / by Hubert Ben Kemoun; translated by
Genevieve Chamberland; illustrated by François Roca.
   p. cm. — (Pathway Books Editions / The Adventures of Sam X)
   ISBN 978-1-4342-0480-6 (library binding)
   ISBN 978-1-4342-0530-8 (paperback)
   [1. Tattooing—Fiction. 2. Snakes—Fiction. 3. Supernatural—Fiction.]
I. Chamberland, Genevieve. II. Roca, François, ill. III. Title.
PZ7.B4248Se 2008
[Fic]—dc22   2007030730

Summary: Sam finds the Great Magic Cobra temporary tattoo in his
cereal. Soon it becomes clear that the tattoo isn't ordinary. It leaves Sam's
arm, and Sam must help it find freedom.

Art Director: Heather Kindseth
Graphic Designer: Kay Fraser

1 2 3 4 5 6 13 12 11 10 09 08

Printed in the United States of America

TABLE OF CONTENTS

CHAPTER 1
The Great Magic Cobra 5

CHAPTER 2
A Snake On My Shoulder 15

CHAPTER 3
Hypnotized. 23

CHAPTER 4
A Monster On the Stairs 35

CHAPTER 5
Under the Wave. 47

Chapter 1

THE GREAT MAGIC COBRA

In October, a new movie came out. It was called "Eddy, Cyclops of the Darkness."

Right after the movie came out, everybody started wearing a firelight. A firelight was a light that you wore strapped to your forehead.

The lights were red or green or blue. They were really cool because they made you look like someone from the future or like a cyclops, with one eye.

My mom laughed when she saw my firelight. "You look like an alien," she teased me.

The firelights stopped being cool right after Christmas. Then, the new trend was to wear brightly colored bandanas.

Candy Roll, the singer, made the bandanas cool when her new CD came out. She wore them all the time. I got a bandana for free when I bought the CD.

My mom didn't tease me about wearing it. She just rolled her eyes.

My friend Lionel wore one on each wrist. Some girls tied their hair back with their bandanas, or wore them tied across their foreheads.

My bandana was bright red. I tied it around my neck, with a knot on one side.

Then in June, something new was cool: temporary tattoos.

We found the tattoos in cereal boxes and gumball machines. The brightly colored designs were easy to put on the skin. You just used a wet washcloth or a sponge.

The tattoos stayed on for three or four days before they started to fade. Then we just rubbed off the rest of the tattoo with some baby oil.

The tattoos looked so real. I scared my mom when she saw a scorpion tattoo on my arm. She started screaming, as if the scorpion had bitten her.

I had to show her the front of the cereal box before she finally calmed down.

Every Tuesday afternoon, a group of my friends went swimming at the pool. Everyone showed off their new tattoos.

Animals were the most popular tattoos. Some kids had big cats with shiny fangs. Some had fire-breathing dragons.

There were other designs in the cereal boxes and gumball machines too. There were flowers, sport cars, and even some star tattoos that glowed in the dark.

But the tattoo everyone wanted was the Great Magic Cobra. No one had found it in their cereal boxes yet.

"I heard there's only one copy of it," Lionel whispered.

We were standing in the locker room at the pool one Tuesday, getting ready for swimming.

"What's so great about a cobra, anyway?" asked Patrick.

Patrick was proud of his Bengal tiger. The tiger tattoo was crawling on his chest.

Lionel looked shocked. "The cobra tattoo is one of a kind!" Lionel exclaimed. "No one else will ever have the same one. Plus, it stays on way longer than the others do."

He shook his head and added, "Are you crazy? The cobra is definitely the best tattoo to get."

Hmm. I guess I had never thought about how cool it really was.

After my scorpion tattoo wore off, I traded two spider tattoos to Charlotte for a Tyrannosaurus Rex. Then I found a daisy in my next box of cereal. I quickly traded that one with Jessie for a dragon.

I was starting to get sort of bored with tattoos. It seemed like I had seen them all.

Then, one Sunday morning, I was pouring myself a bowl of corn flakes. A tattoo floated out of the box. I opened it up. I expected to see another boring tattoo.

But it wasn't boring.

It was the Great Magic Cobra!

I showed it to my mom, but she quickly looked away. "That's disgusting!" she exclaimed as she poured herself a second cup of coffee.

"I just don't understand you kids today," she added. "Why would you want to wear something like that on your skin? Why would you try to make yourself ugly on purpose?" She kept talking, but I stopped listening.

I didn't say anything. I was staring at my snake tattoo. I must have looked like someone who was holding a winning lottery ticket in his hand.

I didn't realize how big the prize would turn out to be.

Rare, Amazing, One of a kind
The Great Magic Cobra
It is waiting for you . . .

Chapter 2

A SNAKE ON MY SHOULDER

The tattoo showed the Great Magic Cobra wrapped around itself. It looked like it was sleeping, with its head lying on its tail. It was twice as big as the other tattoos I'd seen. All of my friends were going to be so jealous.

I stood in front of the bathroom mirror and thought about where I should put the snake tattoo. On my arm? No. The tattoo was too big, and I could already hear my mom freaking out about it.

On my stomach? No. Then I'd have to take off my shirt to show people, and that would be weird.

On my back? No. I couldn't put it on myself.

Plus, if it was on my back, I couldn't see it without looking in a mirror. That would take all the fun out of it. What was the point of having a cool tattoo if you couldn't even see it?

I finally decided that I would put the cobra on my left shoulder. I thought it would make me look kind of like a pirate.

Suddenly, my mom pounded on the bathroom door. I jumped.

"Do you plan on spending the whole day in there?" she called.

"Just give me two more minutes!" I answered.

I pressed the wet washcloth against the tattoo on my shoulder. It was almost done.

"Hurry up!" she said. "I'm running really late." I could hear her footsteps walking quickly away, down the hall.

I hurried up. Then I put my T-shirt back on and left the bathroom. I didn't even have time to check out my new tattoo.

I waited until my mom was in the shower. Then I went into my room and called Lionel. He answered his phone on the first ring.

"What are you doing today?" I asked him.

Lionel sighed. "Nothing special. Some friends of my parents are coming over for the afternoon. It's going to be a really boring day. Do you want to do something?"

I smiled. I didn't care what we did, as long as I could show him my tattoo. I had to show it off!

"Let's meet at the river at three o'clock," I said. "We could go swimming. Oh, and I have something awesome to show you."

Lionel laughed. "Did your mom buy you a pretty new swimming suit?" he joked.

"No," I said. "When I said it was something cool, I wasn't joking. You're going to wish you had what I have. You'll see."

We hung up. I smiled again. Lionel might be laughing now, but he definitely wouldn't be when he got a look at my Great Magic Cobra!

The river is really close to my house. And my mom always says it's okay for me to hang out with Lionel.

"Fine," she said. "Just don't hurt yourself. And be home before dark."

My shoulder itched while I sat at the table eating lunch. That was normal, though, because the tattoo was still getting dry. I thought that it was more itchy than usual, but that was probably because this tattoo was bigger than any other tattoo I'd had.

After I was done eating, I went into the bathroom to look at the tattoo in the mirror. My tattoo was in the perfect spot. The snake's head faced my neck. I had fun making the snake move by rolling my shoulder.

It was amazing. The design looked so real. It seemed like it was alive.

Then I noticed something.

I must not have been paying attention when I put the tattoo on, because I had thought that the snake was sleeping.

But when I looked at it now, I could see that the snake's two huge eyes were open. They were staring right at me.

Weird.

I hopped on my bike and rode quickly to the river. My arm was still itching.

Chapter 3

HYPNOTIZED

When I arrived at the river, Lionel was already there. He was skipping rocks across the water. He ran over when I rode up.

I noticed right away that his tattoo was different. A new blue beetle had replaced the bull that he had on his arm before.

Lionel barely gave me time to lock my bike. He started talking right away.

"So, the cool thing, what is it?" he asked.

I made him wait while I placed my towel on a rock. I didn't say anything.

Lionel was getting mad. "So, what did you have to show me?" he asked, kicking the sand.

I smiled. "Okay, okay," I told him. I took my T-shirt off. "Look at this!" I said.

Lionel's mouth fell open. He didn't say a word. He looked at my shoulder, then at my face, then back at my shoulder.

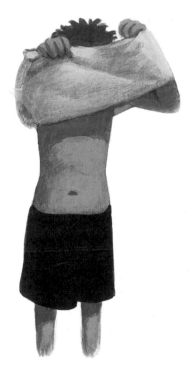

Finally, he said, "You got it! It's the Great Magic Cobra! You're the one who got it!"

I shrugged. "It's just a tattoo," I told him. "It's just a little bigger than the other tattoos, and just a little bit more detailed."

Lionel hit my other shoulder. "Just a tattoo?" he said.

His face was turning red. "Just a tattoo?" he yelled, louder this time.

A fisherman in the river glared at him, but Lionel didn't pay any attention.

"Are you kidding?" he went on. "It's magnificent! Look how its scales are shining under the sun. And its fangs, did you see its fangs? It is the most amazing tattoo I've ever seen!"

Fangs?

I looked at my shoulder. Then I felt a shiver go through my body.

The snake wasn't sleeping. Its eyes were wide open. And two sharp fangs were coming from its open mouth.

"Yeah! Cute little teeth," I said nervously.

I thought I must have been dreaming. The snake was no longer in the same position it had been when it fell out of the cereal box.

That wasn't the only thing that was weird. The snake's head was twice as big as it had been before. And it was staring at me.

"You're so lucky!" whispered Lionel. He just stared at my shoulder.

I frowned. What was going on? Lionel was acting really weird. "Your tattoo is great too," I told him. "Come on. Let's go swimming!"

Lionel didn't answer. He couldn't take his eyes off the cobra. He had a strange look on his face. His eyes were huge and round.

"Lionel," I whispered. "What's wrong?"

No answer. Lionel just stared at my arm.

I reached over and shook his shoulder. "Hey! Lionel!" I said, louder.

He acted like he didn't hear me.

Then I noticed. The cobra was standing up on my shoulder.

The cobra was slowly moving its head from right to left. I could hear a quiet hissing.

The cobra was hypnotizing my friend!

I pushed Lionel down onto a rock so that he would be forced to stop looking at the snake.

"Lionel! Wake up!" I yelled.

Then I grabbed my T-shirt and put it on as fast as I could. The hissing stopped right away.

Lionel shook his head. "What's going on? Where am I? Did I fall?" Lionel mumbled, looking scared.

Lionel looked like he had just woken up from a long nap. He had no idea what was going on.

I sighed. Everything seemed okay. "You slipped from the rock," I told him, trying to hide the truth. "Are you sick?"

Lionel frowned. "I thought I saw a snake. But I couldn't have. It seemed so real, though. Did you see it too?" he asked me.

"Uh . . . yes!" I exclaimed. "It was really scary. It slithered away, though. We're safe now."

I couldn't tell him that he had been hypnotized by my tattoo. That was too crazy.

I peeked under my T-shirt. The cobra was curled up again, sleeping. It was back to its normal tattoo size.

Lionel seemed to have forgotten about the Great Magic Cobra, but I hadn't.

I just had one thing on my mind. I had to get rid of that tattoo.

We decided not to swim after all. There was no way I was going to show my cobra tattoo again. I couldn't risk it.

I told Lionel I was tired and that I had a headache. I thought I should go home. He frowned, but he looked pretty tired too.

Then I hopped on my bike and rode home as fast as I could.

My shoulder was burning. It felt like it was being stung, but how could that be? The itching from the new tattoo should have stopped.

By the time I got home, I really did have a headache. Plus, I was shivering with a fever.

My mom took my temperature. "You have a little fever," she told me.

Then she saw my tattoo. "You kids drive me crazy," she said. "What's the big deal with these tattoos?"

Luckily, the cobra was still asleep.

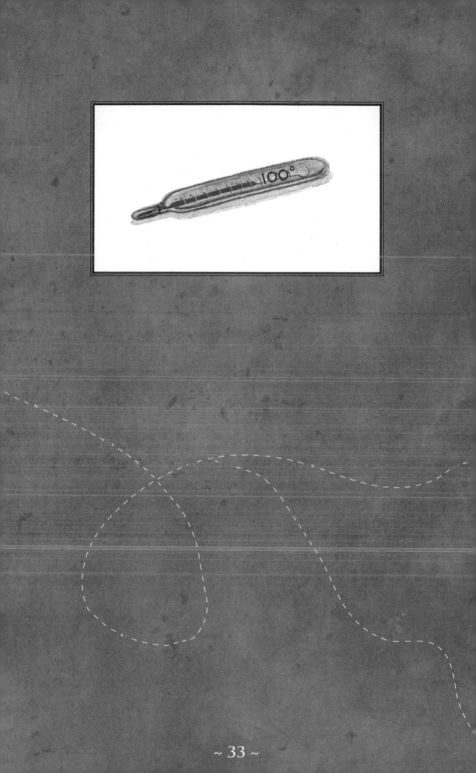

Chapter 4

A MONSTER ON THE STAIRS

I woke up in the middle of the night. I felt awful. My head felt like it was on fire and my shoulder felt like someone was poking it with a fork. I was hot and cold at the same time!

I crawled down the hall to the bathroom to drink a glass of water. Luckily, the cobra was asleep.

I wanted to get rid of the stupid snake once and for all.

I found a washcloth in the hall closet. I got it wet in the sink. Then I rubbed the tattoo for a long time.

Nothing changed. It didn't even look any lighter.

The Great Magic Cobra was the toughest tattoo I had ever had, in more ways than one!

Then I found a sponge with a scratchy side that my mom used for washing the dishes. I thought it might erase the awful snake. I scrubbed extra hard.

But that didn't work either. All it did was make my arm hurt.

Then I saw something. The cobra was staring at me in the mirror.

Was I starting to see things?

The cobra's gaze wasn't scary. It didn't seem mean at all. It just looked at me.

In fact, it looked really sad. Maybe it could tell that I was trying to get rid of it.

The snake stood up on my shoulder, hissing and swaying back and forth.

I wanted to close my eyes. Maybe, if I did, everything would be back to normal when I opened them up again.

But I couldn't close them. I couldn't stop looking at the cobra's eyes. I suddenly started to feel calmer and cooler.

My fever started to go away. My headache started to leave, too.

Suddenly I realized that the snake was hypnotizing me! I knew that I should try to fight it, but it was so soothing. I felt calm and happy.

"Samuel, what are you doing?" my mom asked. She had opened the bathroom door and was looking right at my tattoo.

I jumped and turned around to face her. The hissing stopped right away. Maybe she didn't notice.

I looked in the mirror. The cobra looked like a flat tattoo again. It was asleep on my shoulder.

My mom frowned. Then she reached over and put her hand on my forehead.

"You've cooled off," she said, with her hand on my forehead. "But you're still not going to school tomorrow. Go back to sleep, and I'll wake you up before I leave for work."

She shook her head and frowned at me. "Samuel, I hate this tattoo!" she said. "It scares me!"

I wished I could tell her how much I agreed with her.

* * *

In the morning, when I woke up, my shoulder felt weird again. Even before I looked in the mirror, I could tell the snake wasn't there.

It was gone.

It wasn't on my shoulder, or anywhere else in my room.

I let out a sigh of relief. I was glad the snake was gone. That snake was dangerous. Now I felt a little safer. My headache was gone, and I didn't think I had a fever anymore.

I started to get dressed. But as I was pulling on my shirt, I heard a woman scream. It was a terrible scream.

I knew it was Mrs. Arbin's voice. She was the building caretaker. "Ahhh!" she yelled. "A monster! Help! There's a monster on the stairs! Help! Help! Somebody, please, help!"

A monster?

Quickly, I ran out of our apartment and down the hall. When I got to the stairs, there were three creatures next to Mrs. Arbin's door.

Mrs. Arbin was lying on the floor in front of the elevator. She must have fainted. My giant cobra was heading toward the street. And Norman, Mrs. Aubin's small dog, was barking.

The snake was at least fifteen feet long. It had turned into a real cobra.

The fearless little dog was standing below the snake. It was trying to stop the snake before it could get out of the building.

Norman barked and barked. He jumped onto the cobra's head and bit it.

The cobra hissed. It grabbed the dog in its mouth. I thought the snake would eat Norman. But it didn't. It just tossed the dog into the air while Mrs. Arbin lay there.

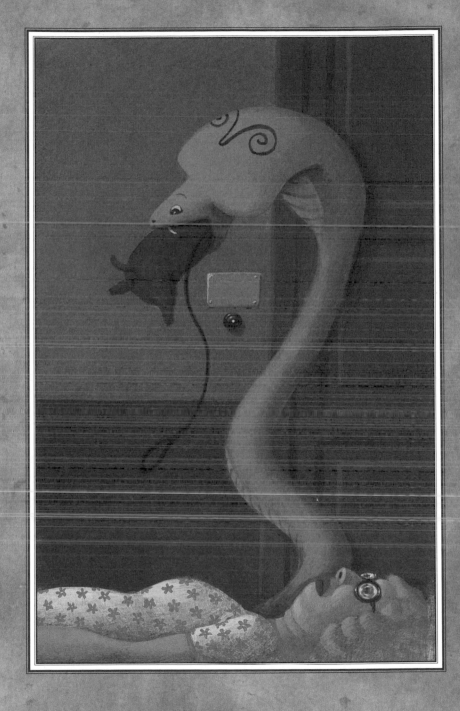

Norman landed on the ground. The dog cried and backed away. Then the snake slowly slid out the front door.

Here's the weird thing. When Norman bit the snake, I felt the bite on my shoulder. I screamed in pain as the cobra slithered quickly away into the street.

Chapter 5

UNDER THE WAVE

It wasn't hard to follow the cobra. I just waited until I heard someone scream. Then I ran toward the noise, knowing that was where the giant snake would be.

There was something else helping me find the snake. It sounds crazy, but I couldn't shake the feeling that I knew exactly how the snake felt. I knew what it was thinking. I knew what was happening to it.

I suddenly realized why the snake had left my shoulder. It knew I wanted to get rid of it, so it escaped before I could do anything.

I was scared of it, of course. But it was still my snake.

By now I could feel how the snake felt. It was trying to find a place to hide.

I knew that if it got hurt, I would feel the pain. Just like how I'd felt it when Norman bit the snake.

What if the snake was killed? Would I die too?

Suddenly I knew what I had to do. I had to help the snake escape.

I rushed to the park on my bike. As soon as I got there, I noticed that people were running away, screaming.

A lady rushed past me and screamed, "Don't go near the fountain! Get away from here!" She kept running toward the exit.

I heard sirens off in the distance. I knew I had to hurry to the fountain.

When I got to the fountain, I saw my cobra, surrounded by statues. It was even bigger now than it had been when it escaped from the apartment building.

It raised its large head. As soon as it saw me standing there, it slithered over to me.

I rubbed the snake's slimy scales. "I can't keep you at home, do you understand?" I told it quietly. "You're way too dangerous. And I think you would make my mom crazy."

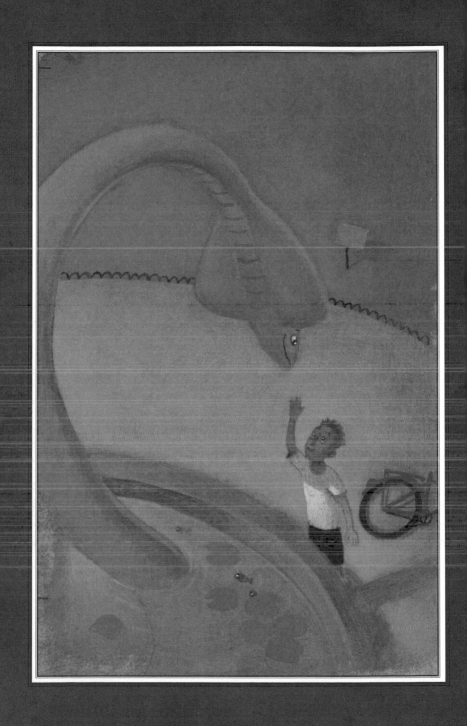

The snake was standing straight up. Its head was sticking out of the water.

It was listening to me. I could tell that it understood me.

Then I saw something terrible.

Five men in weird suits were walking slowly toward the fountain. They were the biggest men I'd ever seen.

One of them was holding a big net. Another one was holding a dart gun.

I had to do something, but what could I do? How could I stop five huge men?

I turned toward the cobra.

"Hurry," I told it. "Get back on my shoulder, as a tattoo. Otherwise, those men are going to get you! Hurry!"

The man who was holding the dart gun moved closer.

"Get away, kid," he yelled at me. He slowly aimed his dart gun at the fountain.

"Hurry! Come back! " I shouted to my snake.

A bullet splashed into the water. At the same time, the snake disappeared.

The men ran over. When they got near me, we could all see that the fountain was empty.

"Where's the monster?" one of the men asked.

I looked at his angry face. Then I said, "It dove under the wave, I think!"

The man smiled. "Good," he said. "It won't be able to live long in the sewer! Now go home, kid."

I left, scratching my shoulder. The itching had started all over again.

The snake was tiny and hiding under my shirt, but it was there. It was a tattoo again.

I hopped on my bike. As I took off down the road, I whispered, "You know, you're probably the first Great Magic Cobra to ride a bike!"

The cobra peeked its tiny head out of my shirt and I heard it hiss. It was enjoying the ride.

It was late afternoon by the time I got to the river. The beach was empty. I took off my shirt and headed for the water.

"Now you can go," I told the snake. "It's safe out here. And if you're ever in danger, you can come back on my shoulder. I'll save the spot for you."

I could already feel the cobra slipping off my shoulder. It was huge. It was a real monster.

The cobra slid farther away. As it swam, it turned to look at me one last time. Then it dove under the waves.

When I got home, my mom was waiting for me.

"I've been trying to call you all day! Where have you been? You are driving me crazy, Samuel!" she said.

Then she hugged me.

I went back to school the next day, and everything was back to normal.

Everyone made fun of me because I didn't have a tattoo. I told them I didn't care. I said that tattoos were boring.

* * *

That was a month ago. Now, our town is famous.

Tourists come from all over the world to our town. They want to take pictures of the river monster. Fishermen say they've seen a monster that's more than 30 feet long. Hunters travel here to try to capture it.

They can try. Every time someone thinks they are about to capture the Great Cobra, it magically disappears.

No one would ever think to look for the Great Cobra on my shoulder.

THE END

ABOUT THE AUTHOR

Hubert Ben Kemoun was born in 1958 in Algeria, on the northern coast of Africa. He has written plays for radio, screenplays for television, musicals for the stage, and children's books. He now lives in Nantes, France with his wife and their two sons, Nicolas and Nathan. He likes writing detective stories, and also creates crossword puzzles for newspapers. When he writes stories, he writes them first with a pen and then copies the words onto a computer. His favorite color is black, the color of ink.

ABOUT THE ILLUSTRATOR

François Roca was born in 1971 in Lyon, France. He studied design, illustration, and communication and went on to illustrate more than 20 children's books in the United States and in his home country, including *The Yellow Train* and *Muhammed Ali: Champion of the World*. Roca is currently working on video games, animated films, and a children's version of King Kong. He now lives in Paris. Roca, that is, not King Kong.

GLOSSARY

bandana (ban-DAN-uh)—a large, brightly colored handkerchief

caretaker (KAIR-tay-kur)—someone whose job it is to take care of a building

cobra (KOH-bruh)—a large, poisonous snake

cyclops (SYE-klahps)—a legendary one-eyed monster

dart gun (DART GUHN)—a special gun that shoots small, pointed objects called darts. The darts can contain a medicine that numbs an animal.

elaborate (i-LAB-ur-it)—complicated and detailed

fangs (FANGZ)—long, pointed teeth

hypnotize (HIP-nuh-tize)—to put someone into a trance

jealous (JEL-uhss)—if you are jealous, you want what someone else has

tattoo (ta-TOO)—a picture that has been printed on someone's skin

MORE ABOUT . . .

- Temporary tattoos aren't real tattoos. They're more like stickers. Some of them can last as long as three weeks!

- The word tattoo comes from a Tahitian word that means "to hit."

- As many as 40 million Americans have tattoos. One third of those are women.

- The electric tattoo machine was invented in 1891 by Samuel O'Reilly of New York City.

- In the past, some sailors tattooed the bottoms of their feet with a pig on one and a rooster on the other. Since these animals don't swim, sailors thought it would help them reach dry land if they ever fell overboard.

. . . TATTOOS

- In 1991, a frozen mummy was discovered in the Alps of Europe. This "iceman" was covered in 57 tattoos.

- Some historians say that Queen Victoria of England, who ruled from 1837 to 1901, had a bracelet tattooed around her wrist.

- According to the *Guinness Book of World Records*, Bernie Moeller has the most tattoos — 14,006! But Tom Leppard, a man from Scotland, has most of his body covered with leopard spots. The only places on his body that are free of tattoos are the inside of his ears and the skin between his toes!

DISCUSSION QUESTIONS

1. In this book, Sam realizes that he feels pain when the cobra feels pain. Why do you think that happens?

2. Sam and his friends go through lots of trends. What are some trends at your school?

3. Why does Sam decide to protect the cobra? What does he do to protect it?

WRITING PROMPTS

1. Pretend that you have a tattoo on your shoulder that has come alive. What is it? What does it do? Write about it and draw a picture of the tattoo.

2. Sometimes it can be interesting to think about a story from another person's point of view. Try writing chapter 3 from Lionel's point of view. What does he think? What does he feel? What does he do and say?

3. Lionel is jealous because Sam has found the rarest tattoo of all. Have you ever been jealous of something a friend had? Write about that time. What were you jealous of? How did you begin to get over it?

INTERNET SITES

Do you want to know more about subjects related to this book? Or are you interested in learning about other topics? Then check out FactHound, a fun, easy way to find Internet sites.

Our investigative staff has already sniffed out great sites for you!

Here's how to use FactHound:

1. Visit *www.facthound.com*

2. Select your grade level.

3. To learn more about subjects related to this book, type in the book's ISBN number: **9781434204806**.

4. Click the **Fetch It** button.

FactHound will fetch the best Internet sites for you!